Forever Loved

Brenda Jenkyns

Illustrations by

Kathy Garren

BMJ Publishing
Calgary, Alberta, Canada
(403) 818-7520

For Ryder Michael

with love,

B.J.

For Simon and Lily

with love,

K.G. (Mimi)

Michael, you will be forever loved

Michael couldn't sleep. It happened every time he worked on an important project. The energy that coursed through his body when he was singing, dancing and planning a show could not easily be turned off when the day was over. It took hours for him to unwind.

For the past few months, this new project had only been a concept in his mind, but tonight at rehearsal, he had finally seen the whole thing come together. It felt good. All the concerts, which were to start in about three weeks, were completely sold out. It amazed and humbled him that so many thousands of people wanted to see him perform after all these years.

His fans had always been his inspiration, as much as he had been theirs. The show he had created for them was beyond anything that had ever been done before. That is what they would be expecting from him, and what he expected of himself.

It had been twelve years since his last concert tour. At that time, outdoor stadiums in fifty-eight different cities around the world had been filled with 50,000 people or more, all singing, swaying and enjoying his one of a kind musical production. His oldest son had been a newborn at the time.

One reason he had chosen to do these concerts now, was because his three children were old enough to appreciate what he did, and he was still young enough to dance and sing the way he always had, from the time he was their age and younger.

He also saw this as another opportunity to use his music to inspire people to love one another, and take care of the planet and the children.

He intended to use these shows to make another one of his dreams come true. Michael Jackson Children's Hospital would be a place where children would be nurtured and loved back to health, as well as being treated with all the benefits of modern medicine.

It would have theatres and games and music, where children could still play, and have fun even though they were sick.

Michael had always believed that joy was an important ingredient in healing, and hospitals were not usually very joyful places.

He had hosted thousands of sick and underprivileged children at his
NEVERLAND VALLEY RANCH
over the years, treating them to a day of carefree fun, which they might not
otherwise have had the opportunity to enjoy.

Michael finally dozed off, just as the sun was coming up.

He opened his eyes, to find himself in a beautiful garden. Trees, shrubs and

beautiful flowers, some he had never seen before, surrounded him.

There were animals, birds and butterflies. Even the breeze seemed to be vibrant and alive. It was the most beautiful place he had ever seen.

Noticing a path winding through the garden, he started walking slowly, taking in the beauty of the peaceful scene.

Looking ahead up the path, he saw someone walking toward him, and he felt a wave of warmth and light flow over him from head to toe.

This person was wearing a long flowing robe and a big smile. The wave of love seemed to be coming from him.

"Michael, my brother," the man said when he was close. He took Michael's hands into his own and squeezed them. His hands were warm and soft and Michael instantly felt safe. Then the man put his arms around him and hugged him close. Michael felt tears running down his cheeks. He never wanted to leave this warm embrace.

Finally, the man held him by the shoulders and looked deeply into his eyes.

"Do you know who I am?" He asked gently.

"Jesus?" Michael knew it was Him. "Why are you here?" he managed to ask.

How many times in his life had he felt Jesus come to his side? Sometimes with a lyric, a melody, a new idea, a feeling of love to comfort him, but this was the first time he had appeared in this way.

"I am here to ask you to come home with me." Jesus said.

"Home?" Michael wondered what that meant.

"You have always given your best in everything you have done, Michael. No one could have asked for more. You chose to follow what you knew in your heart was yours to do, and use your gifts to make a difference. This is a beautiful example for others to live by. Your life's work will live on forever, in your music, your dance and your actions.

Nothing ever stopped you from doing what you knew you were here to do, you never gave up, you never held back, and now it is time for you to rest."

"Rest?" Michael couldn't seem to say more than one word at a time. His life had always been so busy, rest was not a word he associated with himself.

Fifty years - not old, but he had packed so much into those years, he sometimes felt more like eighty. Growing old had never been something he looked forward to. Many people said he had never really grown up at all. He hoped not.

He saw the innocence and wonder of childhood as something to be admired and emulated. Most adults had lost the joy and enthusiasm for life that he had always found in children, and nurtured within himself to keep his ideas new, fresh and unlimited.

Suddenly he realized what Jesus was saying. Come home with him, to heaven, and rest.

Oh, how wonderful that sounded.

To always feel the complete love and joy he felt now.

"But my concerts, I have a commitment," he said softly.

"Yes," Jesus answered. "Your obligations will be met, and your concert will reach more people than you could ever physically perform for. People will have a chance to see you in a way that has not been possible before. They will see the man, the time and effort, the genius, and the commitment and dedication you put into your work. This will help them to understand your message and your purpose, even people who would never have gone to the concerts. Your life's work will capture their attention in a way that has never happened before." Wondering how that could be possible, Michael had another concern.

"My children, they need me."

"Yes, they do need you, and you need them. You will never be separated from them. They will feel your presence and you can share every minute of their lives, guiding them and loving them.

"They really are very wise and capable, beyond their years. You have given them the childhood you wish every child could enjoy. They will remember everything you taught them, and how much you love them. You will be so proud of them."

Michael was silent. His children were his life. Being a father was the most beautiful and fulfilling experience he had ever had. He knew it was not easy for them to have such a famous father. Maybe, in some ways, it would be easier for them without me, the thought floated across his mind. Somehow, he DID feel that he could never be separated from his children. They were his, and he was theirs, forever.

"But there is so much more to be done….." Michael started to say, but Jesus smiled.

"I have a surprise for you Michael, I know your fondest wish is to help ALL children to enjoy their childhood and allow the wisdom of childhood to heal the conflict in the world. What if I told you, that by coming home with me now, you will make an impact on the world that you could never imagine. People everywhere will feel the love that flows from you, entering their hearts to awaken them to their part to play in the healing of the world.

Long forgotten imaginings will be remembered and people will decide to go for their dreams and truly become who they are meant to be, inspired by your example.

You will be able to know each of them individually, like you have longed for and never been able to do in this life. You can inspire them, enjoy their company in dreams, whisper ideas into their ears and delight in their accomplishments, sparked by your message of love.

You are right, there is much more to be done, and you will continue to play your part. They need you now more than ever.

Michael's eyes were wide in amazement. Could it really be possible? It sounded….perfect. A wave of love washed over him again.

"Do you think people will really understand what I have been trying to tell them?" he asked.
"Yes Michael, you are going to be so proud.
Everything you have worked for will be carried on by those who love you,

and the world will come to know what your real message was." Jesus answered with such patience and understanding that Michael started to cry again.

Jesus put his arm around Michael's shoulder and together they turned and walked down the path, into the light.

If Michael has made a difference
in your life, tell us about it at
www.michaeljacksoneverafter.com.
We'd love to hear your story.

1349962R00017

Made in the USA
San Bernardino, CA
12 December 2012